Travel and
Transport

Train is on Track

Peter Bently

Illustrated by

Bella Bee and Lucy Fleming

Train is in the **shunting yard** preparing for a **journey**.

A **shunter** brings the **carriages**.

In the **driver's cab**, Dog checks the **controls**. Then he starts the **engine**.

Train is ready to move to the **platform**.
But why is the **signal** still **red**?

Dog speaks to the **signalman** on his **cab radio.**

"The **express mail train** is in front of you," says the signalman. "It's loading up with all the post!"

At last the mail train leaves and Dog
drives to the **platform**.

Train's doors open and the
passengers **board**.

The **guard** is about to close the doors.

Whirr!
Clunk!

"Wait for me!" cries one late passenger.
She **jumps aboard** just in time!
The doors **close.**

The station manager blows his whistle.

Train pulls out of the station.
"Great, we're on time!" says Dog.

A **goods train** moves into a **siding** to let Train pass. Dog sounds the horn to say **"thank you!"**

TOOT TOOT!

At a **level crossing**, a bell **rings** and lights **flash** as the barriers come down.

Traffic waits for Train to pass.
Everyone **waves** as Train goes by.

After leaving the town, Train goes **faster.**
It **ZOOMS** through the countryside.

A slow train beeps **"Hello!"** as Train
zips through a small station.

WhoOsh!

Train crosses a **steep valley** on a **viaduct**, then **shoots** into a long **tunnel**.

It starts to **rain** and Dog **switches** on the windscreen wiper.

Swish-**SWOOSH!**

Train passes the old branch line. **Steam trains** use it to take **tourists** for rides.

A steam engine **whistles** as Train **whizzes** past.

peep!

The rain gets **worse**. Thunder **crashes** and lightning **flashes**.

Suddenly Dog sees a **red light**. "Yikes! There's another train ahead!"

Dog slams on the emergency brake.
Train **stops** just in time. In front
is the mail train.

scREECH!

A **tree** has **blown over**
onto the **track**.

Nobody is hurt, but the
engine has **derailed**.

Dog **unhitches** the **mail wagon** and **couples** it to the front of Train.

Dog **reverses** Train back to the steam train station.

"Can we use your track?" Dog asks.

"Sure!" says the stationmaster. "We're happy to help!"

The steam train **pulls** into a **siding** so Train can use the **branch** line.

Train heads off down the branch line,
pulling the **mail wagon.**

On the way, Dog sees a
breakdown train lifting the
mail train engine onto a flat truck.

"The post is on time!" says the stationmaster. "Well done, Dog!"

"Thanks," says Dog. "But I couldn't have done it without Train!"

Let's look at
Train

Carriages

Door

Wheel units

Other Rail Vehicles

Shunter

Goods (freight) train

Breakdown train

Steam train

For my family P.B.

Designer: Rachel Lawston
Art Director: Laura Roberts-Jensen
Editors: Tasha Percy and Sophie Hallam
Editorial Director: Victoria Garrard

First published in the UK in 2015 by
QED Publishing
Part of The Quarto Group
The Old Brewery, 6 Blundell Street
London, N7 9BH

www.qed-publishing.co.uk

A catalogue record for this book is available from the British Library.

ISBN: 978 1 78493 024 0

Printed in China